Up on the Hill

Nicola Davies is an author and zoologist. She graduated from Cambridge with a degree in zoology before going on to work in television. Of *Up on the Hill* she says, "Some of the happiest times in my life have been spent with chickens, dogs, and sheep and I know that being with my animals, and caring for them has really got me through some very difficult times. All the children in *Up On The Hill* have got a bit of me in them!" Nicola is also the author of non-fiction books *Poo, Big Blue Whale, Surprising Sharks* and *Ice Bear*.

Books by the same author
Home
Poo: a natural history of the unmentionable
Extreme Animals
Suprising Sharks
Big Blue Whale
Ice Bear

Up on the Hill

Three stories about children in the country

NICOLA DAVIES

Illustrated by Terry Milne

WALKER BOOKS

This is a work of fiction. Names, characters, places and incidents are
either the product of the author's imagination or, if real, are used fictitiously.

First published 2008 by Walker Books Ltd
87 Vauxhall Walk, London SE11 5HJ

2 4 6 8 10 9 7 5 3 1

Text © 2008 Nicola Davies
Illustrations © 2008 Terry Milne

This book has been typeset in Stempel Schneidler

Printed and bound in Great Britain by Cox and Wyman Ltd, Reading

British Library Cataloguing in Publication Data:
a catalogue record for this book
is available from the British Library

ISBN 978-1-4063-0915-7

www.walkerbooks.co.uk

To all the staff and children of Wick Court,
Farms for City Children.

Pretend Cows

One

Maxy sat high up in the biggest apple tree. Mrs Bunting was calling her in to have her tea.

"Maxine! Maxine!" she squeaked.

Maxy chewed thoughtfully on a grass stem and wondered how such a teeny voice could come from such a big, fat body.

Mrs Bunting was getting really cross.

"Maxine! I *know* you can hear me. Come in here *at once*!"

Maxy *was* hungry, and she *did* like Mrs B's teas – lovely gravy and brilliant roast potatoes. But she didn't want to come down from her tree.

At last, the kitchen door slammed. Mrs Bunting had given up. She got into her little car and rattled over the bumps in the farmyard and up the lane, home to give Mr Bunting his tea.

Maxy sighed and leant her cheek against the trunk. It was covered in moss, soft and furry, almost like a teddy. It was comforting to be held in the arms of the tree, up above everything. She could look down on the farm and pretend that it still *was* a proper farm, with cows in the milking parlour and pigs in the sties. But down on the ground she noticed the silence too much, the empty barns, the lost-looking house.

There were no animals on Stelly Farm any more. All the cows and pigs had been killed, shot by vets and soldiers, and then piled in a heap and burned. Daddy had said it had to be done because they *might* be sick and then *might* make animals on neighbouring farms sick too. Maxy couldn't understand it. Anyone could see that all their animals were fine! She wanted to tell the vets that they were wrong, but on the day they came, Mum and Dad sent her away to Nan's.

She had ridden an old bike round and round and round Nan's tiny garden until it got dark and Nan had made her come inside. The next day, when Nan took her home, the yard had been hosed and the barns swept; there wasn't a trace of an animal to be seen. Even their smell faded after a while. Maxy snuffled in corners to find the last familiar whiffs of pig or cow.

Dad had to work away after that, milking a big herd of cows belonging to a farmer on the other side of the county. He left before Maxy woke and often got back after she was asleep. Mum worked harder too, cycling off down the lane to the village every morning to clean people's houses. Sometimes Maxy went to Nan's after school, and sometimes Mrs Bunting came and cooked her tea and squeaked around the kitchen until Mum got home.

Everything was sad without the animals and the daily routine of feeding and milking. Moping round the empty farm was boring, so Maxy found a way to make herself feel better: Pretend Cows. She would walk out into the fields and bring the herd of Pretend Cows into the yard, ready for milking, just as she'd done with the real ones. It felt nice to shout the names of her old favourites and to scold them like she used to do.

"C'mon, Patch, pick your feet up. That's my gal, Ella. Get on there, Daze!"

In some ways, Pretend Cows were better than real ones, because Pretend Cows only needed attention when the weather was fine.

Sometimes, when the Pretend Cows were being milked, Maxy would stand at the door of the milking parlour. She'd imagine the *shlump, shlump, shlump* of the milking machine and the sound of her dad singing along to the radio as he worked.

Little by little, things began to get a bit better. Dad got a job nearer the farm and sometimes came home for tea. He began to talk about "restocking", buying new animals and starting again. At Christmas, Mum and Dad talked about "making plans" and smiled secretly at each other over the turkey. At Easter, they told her that she would be having a little brother or sister in the summer. Maxy told them that was OK but that she'd rather have cows and pigs on the farm than a baby. Mum

12

and Dad laughed, and Mum said that maybe by the summer they'd have a baby *and* animals!

When spring came all the Pretend Cows had twins, and there was even a Pretend Pig and ten Pretend Piglets in the end sty. Things were definitely looking up! But then Mum got ill and had to go to hospital, and Maxy started living up the apple tree.

Two

Maxy woke in Dad's arms. He was carrying her down the ladder, out of the tree.

"Why can't I sleep up there?" she whined sleepily.

"Because you're not a monkey. Now don't wriggle, else we'll both fall!"

It was cold now. The sky was streaked with purple and dotted with the first stars. Maxy let Dad hold her tight and carry her right across the yard and into the warm kitchen.

He dolloped her into a chair, wrapped in his sweater.

"Mmmm. Mrs Bunting's teas!" he said. "Want some?"

Maxy nodded. The gravy was a bit crusty round the edges, but it still tasted good. Dad and Maxy ate it all up.

"Ahh," said Dad, leaning back in his chair. "That's better! So, what did you do after school today?"

"Milking, of course!" Maxy said. How could Dad forget that? It amazed her. Dad looked at the floor and ran one hand through his hair. It didn't do any good, Maxy noticed, it stayed just as spiky and wild as ever.

"Oh," he sighed. "The pretend cows again."

"Yes. The *cows*," said Maxy, sticking out her chin. "Milk yield's down and Stella's limping badly on her right hind foot. But we don't need the vet because I put a poultice on it earlier!"

Dad opened his mouth to say something, then shut it again.

"Is there any pudding?" asked Maxy.

She ate one slice of pie and Dad ate two, and almost all the custard. Then they sat together and listened to the bubbling sound the range always made at night.

After a while, Dad cleared his throat and said, "I went to see Mum tonight, Maxy."

Maxy knew he'd been to the hospital because he'd changed out of his work overalls and put on a clean shirt, but she didn't say anything.

"D'you want to know how she was?"

Maxy looked up at the ceiling. She didn't want to look at Dad. He might *say* Mum was all right, but that couldn't be true because she was in hospital.

Maxy looked harder at the ceiling: there was a crack around the light fitting that looked just like a drawing of a wing or the edge of a pie or perhaps a beehive.

"She's much better, Maxy," Dad's voice went on. "And the baby's very nearly ready to be born!"

He sounded really excited, but Maxy still didn't want to look at him. Dad *said* it was OK. But it might not be and Maxy didn't want to think about that at all. That was why she had never been to see

Mum in hospital. So she stared straight at the light bulb. At first it was white, then yellow and then a kind of blobby pink, filling up her eyes and burning everything else away.

"I'm going to bed now, Dad," Maxy said. "I need to be up early to look at that poultice."

Three

The next day, Nan picked Maxy up from school. She said that Dad had taken an afternoon off and was waiting for her at home!

Maxy didn't say anything. Nan was sure to be wrong, she was always getting in a muddle about things. Mrs Bunting would be waiting, not Dad. So Maxy made plans to check on the Pretend Cows and then to scoot up the apple tree.

But Nan was right. Dad *was* in the yard, busy

putting the finishing touches to a new chicken coop.

"What's that for?" Maxy asked.

"Bantams," Dad said. "You know, Maxy, little chickens. Good layers, and good broodies too."

"Why?"

"I thought some proper fresh eggs would be good for your mum and the baby."

Maxy walked all around the coop. Dad had done a great job. There was a little house at one end with a sloping tin roof and a door that slid open when you pulled a string. There was a box at the back of the house, with a lid to lift to collect the eggs, and a run at the front, covered in wire to give the bantams a safe place to scratch about.

Dad nailed a latch on the lid of the egg box.

"That's it. It's ready. Will you help me carry it, Max?"

"I don't know," Maxy said. "It's nearly time to bring the cows in."

"I know, but this won't take a minute. We can put it on the grass by the appl⸱ tree."

Maxy took the light end, and they carried the coop across the yard together.

"Which way round would the chickens like best?" Maxy asked.

"I'm not sure. What do you think?"

Maxy thought for a minute.

"They'd like the morning sun, so they can warm up quick if it's been cold at night."

"Good idea," said Dad. "So they should face the house?"

Maxy nodded.

"When will you get the chickens?"

"Oh," said Dad. "Pretty soon."

Ha! Maxy knew what *that* meant! He'd been saying the same thing for months about when they'd be getting some more cows. Maxy glared at him but he didn't seem to notice.

"Hadn't you better check on Stella's bad leg?" he said, with a big smile. Dad never asked about the Pretend Cows, he was just trying to get rid of her so she wouldn't ask about the stupid bantams any more. She didn't bother to tell him that Stella was fine now, and had given birth to triplets!

She turned and ran off into the first field, calling "Stella! Daze! Marty! C'mon now!"

The Pretend Cows were behaving very badly.

The calves kept running off, and even the grown-ups were skittish and wouldn't go where Maxy wanted them to. Maxy gave up. Might as well be up the apple tree, she thought.

Just as she got within sight of the tree, a very loud noise came from Dad's coop. "Cooockkodddooodleoooooooo!"

Maxy raced up to take a closer look. There, strutting in the new run, as if he'd owned it *forever*, was a perfect little cockerel! He had glossy chestnut feathers that flashed purple and blue where they caught the light. They were brightest at his throat, where they shone and billowed like a silk scarf, and on his tail, where they shot up like a rainbow fountain. Maxy could see that he knew how beautiful he was. He swaggered up and down the run, tossing his head and making his bright red comb flop over one eye.

Dad came and stood beside her.

"I didn't know soon was now!" said Maxy.

Dad grinned. "What should we call him?" he asked.

Maxy thought of an old pop star she'd seen on TV once, someone who'd been famous even before *Dad* was born. *He'd* wiggled just like this cockerel and had a floppy fringe like the cockerel's droopy comb.

"Elvis!" said Maxy. "That's his name!"

Dad laughed out loud and ruffled her hair with his hand.

"Well, let's see if Elvis likes the wives I've got him."

He reached into the cardboard box at his feet and pulled out a squawking bundle of feathers, which he shoved, quickly, into the run through the little door at its end.

The bundle turned out to be three hens, bunched up together. They stepped apart and shook their feathers. Two of them reminded Maxy of Nan's tea cosy. They were round and homely, with soft fluffy feathers that looked like fur. One was brown and the other was white, but they both had a spot of blue skin on their cheeks, like a tiny patch of sky.

"They're silkies," said Dad. "Your mum kept silkies when she was a girl. They're the best mums. They sit tight on their eggs no matter what, until they hatch."

"What'll we call them?" Maxy asked.

"Coffee and Cream?" said Dad.

Maxy nodded.

Elvis started showing off to Coffee and Cream immediately. Maxy could see that they were only pretending to ignore him. But the third hen really was ignoring all Elvis's fine feathers and strutting about. She stood at the end of the run and stared up into the branches of the apple tree.

"She's a cross-breed," said Dad. "Her mum was a Partridge Wyandotte but her dad was a duck-winged Old English Game."

Maxy nodded as if she knew all about wire-pots and duck-games. Whatever she was, Maxy liked the look of the third hen. There was nothing rounded or fluffy about her at all. She had long legs and smooth grey feathers that fitted her closely. She had proper wings too, with long black feathers, folded neatly to her sides. Her eyes were bright and her comb was small and tidy, like a cap. She looked ready for anything.

"Her eggs will be pretty tiny," said Dad. "But she was free, so I'm not grumbling! What d'you want to call her?"

"I don't know yet. I'll have to get to know her a bit."

"Fair enough," said Dad.

Dad filled the chickens' special water holder from the tap in the yard and fetched layers' pellets for them, from the feed store where they used to keep the cows' food. Then he and Maxy stood with the afternoon sun on their backs, watching the four birds get used to their new home.

Elvis and the two silkies were settling in together nicely, pecking from the feeder and taking turns to sip water. But the third hen had turned her back on them and was pacing up and down the run. She didn't look very happy.

"Don't worry," Dad said. "She'll feel at home once she's laid an egg here!"

But Maxy wasn't so sure.

"I'm going to keep watch, to make sure she's all right," said Maxy. "From up the tree."

Dad sighed. He looked disappointed.

"Will you come down for supper?" he asked.

"Maybe," said Maxy.

Four

The next morning there was a note on the kitchen table, written on the back of an old envelope with one of Maxy's crayons, a pink one.

Had to go to work extra early.
Cow having a difficult birth.

EAT BREAKFAST!!!

Nan will pick you up at 8.30.

Be ready.
Love
Dad

P.S. Please can you check on the bantams? Fetch eggs!

It was a lovely warm morning. The sun was shining right on the chicken coop. Looking out of the kitchen window, Maxy could see the bantams scratching about already. She put her cereal into a big mug, to make it easy to carry, got a spoon from the drawer and headed outside to have breakfast with the chickens.

Elvis, Coffee and Cream clucked hopefully when she sat down on the grass by the coop. They knew that human visitors meant easy food. They watched her through the mesh for a few moments, but when they worked out she wasn't going to share her cereal, they went back to pecking their pellets.

It took Maxy a moment to spot the third hen (she still hadn't thought of a name for her); she was dust-bathing in a little dip of bare earth. Her feathers were ruffled, fluffed out, so that she looked soft and scruffy. She rolled and shuffled, so that the dusty earth flew up around her and caught the light like gold, but when she saw Maxy watching her, she popped up onto her skinny legs and shook herself smooth. Maxy didn't know if hens could be embarrassed, but she certainly looked as though she was.

The hen began scratching furiously at the ground then staring fiercely at the place she'd disturbed, looking for worms. She found one almost at once; it writhed in her beak, looking as big as a snake against her tiny body. It looked far too much for the hen to swallow, but she managed it, gulping hard and squeezing her bright eyes tight shut in concentration. At last the worm was gone. Maxy thought the hen looked a bit sick, like someone who'd eaten two of Mrs Bunting's teas. But a moment later she chased a fat bluebottle around the run and leapt like a goalie going for a save to catch it in her beak. Maxy wanted to cheer.

Watching the hen was so interesting that Maxy didn't hear Nan's car pull into the yard, and only noticed her when she sat down on the grass.

"Hi," said Nan. "Nice chooks! What's that little one called?"

"I don't know," sighed Maxy. "I can't decide. She's too fierce and clever for an ordinary name."

"Minerva," said Nan. "She was the goddess of wisdom, Greek or Roman or something; I don't recall. Anyway, dead clever."

"Minerva. OK," said Maxy. "I like it!"

Nan smiled and got up. "Good," she said. "OK, Maxy. Time to go!"

"Wait!" said Maxy. "I forgot about the eggs!"

She ran to the nest box at the back of the pen and gently lifted the lid. Nestling in the straw were two white eggs. They were a bit smaller than normal hens' eggs, but plump and cosy-looking; just the sort of eggs you'd expect the fluffy silkies to lay! Maxy looked for Minerva's egg; it would be really small, and quite pointy too, she thought. But there was nothing. In spite of dust-bathing and worm-swallowing, the little chicken didn't feel at home enough to lay.

Five

The good weather didn't last the day. By the time Nan dropped Maxy off after school it was blustery, cold and raining. Mrs Bunting was waiting in the yard with an umbrella. She took Maxy's hand and marched her to the kitchen door.

"You're not climbing up trees with a storm brewing, young lady. A good tea is what you need."

Maxy didn't bother arguing. She sat at the table

while Mrs Bunting clattered saucepans on the range, then put the plate of food in front of her. It was her favourite, lamb with buttery carrots, roast potatoes and Mrs Bunting's lovely gravy. Maxy suddenly felt very bad about hiding up the tree so many times.

"Thank you, Mrs Bunting," she said in a small voice.

"That's all right, my duck," Mrs Bunting said softly. "Just you eat up now." She patted Maxy, just once, on the shoulder. Maxy smiled at her, then ate until her plate was clean.

Mrs Bunting and Maxy did the washing up, then it was time for Mrs B to go. Maxy stood at the door to say goodbye.

"Your dad'll be home in an hour," said Mrs Bunting. "So you stay inside, out of the weather, all right?" Maxy nodded. Mrs Bunting got in her car.

"I like your little chooks," she said before she closed the door. "Fresh eggs, that's just what your mum'll need when she comes home, to build up her strength. Shame she can't get them in that hospital, food's all out of a packet there. Bye now." The car door slammed and Mrs Bunting clattered off down the lane.

Maxy stood in the quiet kitchen and stared at the two white eggs in the bowl. It was no good sending raw eggs to hospital, but hard-boiled ones would be OK. She took a small saucepan out of the cupboard and filled it with cold water, then she put the eggs in the water and set it on the range. She didn't know how long it took to hard-boil eggs, so she left them bubbling away while she fetched her crayons and some paper.

Maxy drew a picture of the new coop, with Elvis, Coffee and Cream standing together in the run. Minerva was standing on top of the drinker with a massive wriggly worm in her beak. There was blue sky over the apple tree, and the sun was shining. Then she thought very hard about the Pretend Cows, and while she was thinking, she wrote, "To Mum" very fast, at the top of the picture.

Maxy made a case for the eggs from an old egg box. She crayoned patterns all over it and wrote "hard boiled" in big letters on the lid.

When that was done, she took the pan off the stove and spooned the cooked eggs into the decorated egg box. For a moment she felt pleased, but then she noticed how lonely the two eggs looked in the box, with four empty spaces beside them. How much better they'd look with just one more egg, a very special little egg, from a very fierce little chicken! Maybe by now Minerva had laid an egg.

The wind was blowing hard, slapping the rain into Maxy's face as she crossed the yard. The weather had driven the chickens to roost already; none of them were out in the run. Maxy lifted the egg box lid a crack and felt about inside; no eggs, nothing but straw. She lifted the lid a little more, so she could look inside and be sure she hadn't missed a little egg. In the dimness of the roost Maxy saw Elvis was on the perch, with Cream under his left wing and Coffee under his right. She was just thinking how sweet this was, when Minerva popped out of the shadows. Her eyes were brighter than ever, and she moved quickly. Before Maxy had the chance to even think, the little chicken was out under the open lid, and into the air! She wasn't a very good flyer, and she had to flap very hard to move at all, but she managed to get up into the apple tree. Maxy could see her, high in the branches, clinging on tight in the wind and already soaked and bedraggled by the rain. Maxy had to get her down! She was so tiny. How could she survive a night out in the storm?

She began to climb the apple tree, but the trunk was slimy with rain and wellies were no good for climbing. She was on her fourth try when Dad got home. He ran through the puddles towards her. Maxy could see he was very cross.

"How could you be so silly? Tree-climbing in a storm! Get inside this instant!"

Back inside, Maxy explained about Minerva's escape. She didn't say anything about the third egg, but Dad saw the picture and the egg box on the table and stopped being so cross. He told her to have a hot bath and get ready for bed.

When she came down in her pyjamas, he hadn't got changed, ready to go to the hospital. He was still sitting at the table in his work clothes, looking at her picture.

"I thought I'd give the hospital a miss tonight," he said. "Mum'll be fine without me for an evening."

Maxy looked at Dad's face. He was tired, but he wasn't scared. Maxy smiled at him. Maybe Mum really would be fine.

"Shall I take her your picture tomorrow night?" Dad asked quietly.

Maxy nodded. "And the eggs," she said.

"Yes, and the eggs," said Dad.

The storm rattled the windows and buffeted the door. Dad made some hot chocolate and they sat sipping and listening to the wind racing around the yard. Maxy worried about Minerva.

"Will she be safe up the tree?"

"She'll be fine, don't you worry," said Dad. "And she'll be so hungry in the morning that she'll eat out of your hand."

Maxy didn't believe him but she was too sleepy to argue.

Six

Maxy was dreaming. She dreamt the storm had blown itself out and quiet moonlight streamed into her room from a clear, starry sky. Dad came in and sat on her bed. Even in the dark she could tell he was smiling and smiling.

"I have to go, Maxy," he said. "The baby's being born. It'll be here by the morning. Nan's come to sleep in the spare room." Then he got up and left. Maxy filled up with a warm, lovely feeling that she couldn't name at first. Then she said to herself, "It's happiness, that's what it is!"

So she lay on her dream bed, which was just like a real one, and felt very happy. She looked through the window at the moon sailing in the sky. The light was so bright. Outside there would be moonshadows, and everything would be lit up in blue and silver. The fields, the barns, the apple tree … and the little chicken asleep in its branches.

Maxy got up in her dream. Then she slipped downstairs and out into the yard.

Everything was as clear as day, shiny with the rain and glinting like glitter on a Christmas card. All the puddles were made of melted moonshine and every tiny pebble had been dipped in silver. She crossed the yard as quietly as she could and stood at the bottom of the apple tree, listening. There was only one sound: a faint purring from the chicken roost. Dream chickens purring in their sleep. Maxy smiled to herself and began to climb. It was still a bit slippery but easy to climb in bare feet.

She reached her favourite place, the Y where a big branch met the trunk. She looked up into the branches, all very white and very black in the moonlight. There was no sign of Minerva. Maxy stepped into the Y, ready to climb higher, and almost stepped on the tiny chicken. She had cuddled up to the trunk, just as Maxy had done so many times, and she was fast asleep with her head tucked under her wing. She didn't even stir when Maxy picked her up and tucked her safely inside her pyjama top for the climb down.

Maxy felt inside the roost for the warm fluffy shapes of Elvis and the silkies, then she put Minerva next to them on the perch, cuddled up cosy and safe. Just as Maxy let the little bantam go, she purred a tiny squeaky purr and snuggled deeper under her own wing.

Maxy tiptoed back across the yard, afraid to make a sound and somehow spoil the silent, silvery dreamworld. She went back to bed, curled up like a sleepy bantam and shut her eyes.

Seven

Maxy woke feeling funny. There was something she was supposed to remember but she couldn't think what it was. Was there a school trip today she'd forgotten about? Was it somebody's birthday, but she couldn't think who? It was light outside but the sky was still dawn-pink. Too early even for Dad to be up. She crept downstairs to look for clues.

The picture and the egg box had gone from the

table. Maxy couldn't work out why. She got herself a drink of orange juice from the fridge and noticed that her hand left a dirty mark on the carton. She was filthy: hands, feet, pyjamas. It didn't make any sense... and then she remembered the feel of the wet bark under her bare feet. The glittery shininess of her midnight adventure shot through Maxy all at once like a silver arrow. She threw open the kitchen door and ran over the yard to the apple tree and chicken coop.

She was in a daze. The pink early morning sky and the moonlight glow of the night whirled round inside her, real and dream and pretend all mixed up together. She wanted it all to be true, the baby and Mum, and Minerva all safe; but maybe it was only as real as Pretend Cows.

Elvis, Coffee and Cream were scratching in their little yard, but Minerva was nowhere to be seen. Maxy felt the tears prickling her eyes. She lifted the lid of the egg box a little and looked inside. Staring up at her, bold and fierce, was the little hen! She was sitting cosily in the straw, but when she saw Maxy she jumped up clucking and went out into the run. Maxy looked down at where Minerva had been sitting. There, beside the two fat little eggs, was a much smaller one, deep brown and speckled.

Maxy wanted to shout with happiness. She flew back to the house and fetched the quilt from her bed. Then she wrapped it around herself and sat down outside the kitchen door. All she had to do now was wait.

It didn't take long. At six o'clock Nan opened her bedroom curtains, and a moment later Dad's car pulled into the yard! Dad rushed towards Maxy and hugged her as if his life depended on it. Then Nan ran out of the kitchen in her dressing gown and hugged them both.

"You've got a baby brother!" Dad said to Maxy.

"And I've got a grandson," said Nan.

"Is Mummy all right?" Maxy asked.

"Yes, love," said Dad gently. "Fine. Eating hard-boiled eggs when I left her!"

Maxy gave the biggest sigh.

"Can we go and see them?" asked Maxy.

Dad smiled a funny, rainy smile, his eyes full of tears.

"Yes, we can."

"Just as soon as we've had breakfast!" said Nan.

"Good!" said Maxy. "There's one egg each!"

The
Littte Mistake

One

Rose raced up the sloping yard to the farmhouse at top speed. She kicked off her wellingtons, ran down the hall and skidded into the kitchen door with a bang.

"People usually open doors first, Rose," said Dad through a mouthful of chips.

"She's probably lost her teddy," added Robert, and they both laughed. Sometimes Rose didn't like her dad and her big brother at all, and she was just about to tell them so, when she felt a hand on her shoulder; it was Mum.

"What's the rush, Rosie Posie?" she said. "I saw you tearing up the yard like a rabbit."

Mum's face was a whole nest of wrinkles, but her dark eyes were as bright and alive as a robin's.

"Trixie's in the barn," Rose told her. "I think she's having her puppies!"

"Is she now!" Mum grinned. Trixie's pups were famous for miles around as the best sheepdogs in the county, and Mum was just as excited as Rose was about the new litter. "Well, we'd better go and check on her!" said Mum.

"Can we have your chips, then?" Dad and Robert called after them. Mum rolled her eyes.

"Those boys!" she said. "What are they like?"

Mum collected the Puppy Bag from the hall cupboard. Inside was a lantern in case the birth lasted into the night and a medical kit to help Trixie or her pups if the birth was a difficult one.

"Don't know why I bother taking it, though," Mum laughed. "Trixie never needs help."

Two

Mum and Rose slipped quietly in through the barn door and closed it behind them. The white flash on Trixie's nose showed in the dim light. She was lying on the floor, where she had swirled the hay into a kind of nest.

"How many pups d'you think she'll have this time?" Rose asked.

"She's old now, so maybe only three or four," said Mum. "But one of them could still be a champion!"

Some of Trixie's pups had won prizes at the county sheepdog trials. But as this would be her last litter, Mum had found an extra special mate for her, a fine collie dog called Bullet. Mum and Rose had high hopes for the puppies.

Trixie wagged her tail weakly and licked Mum's hand but then lay still. Every few seconds she gave a little grunt as her tummy muscles tightened to help squeeze the puppies out.

"Won't be long now," said Mum. "She must have got to the barn just in time!"

Rose and Mum stroked Trixie's head and comforted her during her contractions, expecting any minute to see the first little wet bundle of puppy appear from Trixie's bottom.

But no puppies came. Blackbirds sang their last songs in the spring dusk. It grew dark and Rose lit the gas lantern, but still no puppies came.

Trixie began to look very tired.

"Poor old girl," said Mum, "let's see what's happening, shall we?"

Mum had helped with hundreds of litters of puppies. The vet always said she knew more about dogs giving birth than he did. She put a surgical glove on her right hand and very gently felt inside Trixie. Rose held a torch to give her extra light.

"Oh dear," said Mum. "No wonder you've had so much trouble, Trix. These pups are huge."

Mum pulled out one pup and then another. They were both dead. Rose didn't want to look at them. She was glad Mum put the bodies straight behind a bale, where Trixie wouldn't see them. Rose bit her lip. She knew she had to be brave. Crying now wouldn't help.

"There's just one more to come," said Mum. "But it's even bigger. I'm going to have to pull hard. Keep the torch steady now, Rose."

Mum got hold of the pup, and the next time Trixie had a contraction, she pulled. Trixie seemed to know that Mum was trying to help, and put every bit of strength she had left into pushing.

"Come on, Trix!" Mum said.

Then there was a slurping sound, and it was over. Trixie went limp, Mum fell back on the hay and Rose sat down in a heap.

The only one of them who seemed full of life was the puppy. It lay in a wet dollop on the hay, still half-covered in the see-through sac of skin that had held it safe in Trixie's tummy. It squirmed and let out a loud squeak. At once, Trixie turned to the pup and began to lick it. Her strong pink tongue pummelled and pounded its body, like hands kneading dough. The puppy squeaked more loudly, but its little voice kept being smothered by Trixie's licking. It sounded like someone trying to whistle underwater.

"There's no doubt it's alive," said Mum. "Though what sort of dog it is I don't know."

Now that the puppy was clean, Rose could see that it didn't look anything like a sheepdog. Instead of being black and white with sleek smooth fur, its coat was pale and rough, like dirty wool.

"I don't know whose puppy you are," Mum told it. "But you certainly aren't Bullet's. Trixie must have slipped off and mated with another dog on the sly. Oh, Trix!"

Mum sounded so disappointed, Rose was glad that it was dim enough in the barn to hide the hot blush that spread over her face; this pup was her fault. The day before Bullet had been brought to mate with Trixie, Rose had taken her for a walk.

"Don't let her off the lead," Mum had said, but Trix whined so much that Rose had given in and let her run free. The moment she was free, Trixie disappeared. Rose had called and called, but Trix didn't come back for two hours. That must have been when it had happened!

It was almost midnight. Trixie had taken six hours to give birth to one funny-looking puppy that would never win anything at all! Mum looked sadly at the fuzzy white body, cuddled up to Trixie's belly.

"Bit of a mistake, aren't you, pup?" she told it, and shook her head.

Three

Rose woke early. Outside she could hear Dad and Robert driving the tractors and trailers off down the lane. They worked together for all the other farms around and about, cutting grass to make into silage, winter feed for cattle and sheep. They would be gone until well after dark.

Sunshine poured in through her window and birds sang. It was going to be a lovely day. But instead of bouncing out of bed as usual, Rose crept from under the duvet, slow as a slug, with a cold puddle of guilt and disappointment sloshing inside her.

Mum was in the kitchen when Rose went down. She liked "a bit of peace" first thing, so Rose made herself a plate of toast and sat listening to the tocking of the old clock on the dresser. At last, Mum spoke.

"Shame about that pup," she said.

Rose knew now was the time to tell Mum that Trixie's odd pup was all her fault. But instead she cut her toast into four perfect triangles and looked at her plate.

After breakfast, Mum sent Rose to feed Trixie. Inside the barn, streaks of sunlight made the dust dance in the air over the dog's head.

"Here you are, girl," said Rose. Trixie opened her eyes and sniffed at the bowl. She struggled to her feet, gulped the food down in ten seconds, then lapped a whole bowl of water. The pup was fast asleep in the nest of hay. Trixie seemed to understand that Rose could be babysitter, so she slipped outside to wee on the grass at the back of the barn.

While she was gone, Rose looked at the pup. Curled up with its blunt baby nose tucked into its stubby puppy tail, it looked sweet. Its coat was a mass of little fluffy curls the colour of whipped cream, its legs were long and its paws looked as if they were several sizes too large. Rose knew that puppies grew into their paws, so it was clear this pup was going to be a very big dog indeed. She couldn't imagine who the dad had been.

The pup was dreaming. Its paws were moving and its body was twitching. Whatever could a newborn pup dream about, Rose wondered. Perhaps it was dreaming about the life it was going to have. Rose reached out and touched the pup gently on its head.

"A bit of a mistake."

Once, long ago, Mum had said almost the same thing about her! Rose had been too small to talk then, but she remembered hearing Mum telling Aunty Sylvia.

"Rose was our little mistake," she'd said. *Our little mistake;* what did it mean, Rose wondered? It didn't seem very nice to begin your life as a mistake.

Trixie came back and lay down next to her sleeping baby.

"I like your pup, Trix," Rose whispered. Trixie licked the back of Rose's hand, then laid her head on her paws and went to sleep.

Four

Just as they were about to leave for school, Mum's mobile rang. It was Dad; the big tractor had broken down and he needed her to bring him some tools and spare parts.

"I'll drop you at school and go straight there," Mum said. "Don't know what I'll do about the shearer though. He's due here at ten-thirty and I won't have time to get the sheep penned for him."

Mum's face creased in worry. It was hard to get

the shearer to come to a small flock like theirs; somehow they *had* to be ready. Before she'd even thought it, Rose said, "I'll get the sheep penned, Mum."

"Are you sure, Rosie Posie?"

Rose wasn't really sure but it seemed too late to say that now.

"I know what to do."

Mum frowned, then smiled.

"All right. Give it a try."

"I can be a bit late for school, can't I?"

"Of course," said Mum. "I'll write you a note."

Rose let Bobby, Mum's second sheepdog, out of her pen in the first of the old stable boxes. Bobby was one of Trixie's daughters, bigger and stronger than her mum, but not as bold or swift. She bounded around Rose's legs, delighted to be out in the sunshine. Rose was nervous. Mum had taught her how to work with sheep and dogs as soon as she was big enough to walk and blow into a whistle, but she'd never done it without Mum standing by. Rose bit her lip; she had to do this job well, to make up a little bit for Trixie's pup. She took a deep breath.

"C'mon, Bobby!" she said.

As Rose and Bobby neared the gate to the meadow, Bobby grew quiet and sharp. Like all good sheepdogs, she knew that once in the field she was on duty.

Lord's Meadow was on the steepest bit of hillside, with bracken and brambles in clumps around its edges. The flock was at the very top, grazing busily. Rose's job was to get the sheep into the pen in the shady corner, by the gate.

Mum's flock was small, just twenty ewes and their lambs, but once there had been more than two thousand sheep on Ridge Farm.

"They filled the whole yard on shearing day," Mum had told her. There was an old photo on the dresser of a young Mum and Dad and a very small Robert standing in a sea of woolly backs, with big grins on all their faces. But something had gone wrong. When Rose was just a month old, the big

flock was sold, and Dad took to working with machines instead of sheep. No one talked about it, but Rose wondered if her birth had somehow brought bad luck to Ridge Farm. Was that what Mum had meant by "Rose was our little mistake"?

Rose and Bobby stepped into the field. Rose looked down at Bobby. The dog was staring up at the sheep, trembling with energy, absolutely dying to get going. Rose felt better; at least Bobby knew what to do!

The little flat whistle tasted of Mum's face cream. It was cold on Rose's lips. She took a big breath and blew. The sound was almost too high to hear, but Bobby knew just what it meant. She set off like a rocket, a blur of black and white streaking over the bright grass.

Rose blew again, to steady the dog. If she ran straight at the sheep they'd panic and scatter, and then it would take all morning to get them penned.

The trick was to keep them calm, moving together in a tight flock. But Bobby was too excited, and Rose had made her command too late. Bobby raced up to the sheep and they ran in all directions.

"Lie down! Lie down!" Rose yelled. Bobby dropped to the ground and lay with her ears flat to her head. The sheep stood, nervous and staring, ready to bolt again. Rose held her breath. Slowly, they calmed, put their heads down and began to graze.

Mum always said that working a dog with sheep was like tuning into a radio station: you had to find the place where the signal was crystal clear.

"It's all about paying attention, Rose," Mum had said. "You have to concentrate." Rose put the whistle to her lips again and concentrated hard, watching Bobby carefully so that her commands came at just the right moment. Now, when she whistled, the dog reacted at once, trotting backwards and forwards across the slope of the field, gently pushing the flock towards the pen. Rose felt a tingle, as if an invisible thread ran through the shining air between her and the sheepdog.

The last stretch before the pen was tricky. One of the ewes startled and stood tense, all set to run in panic. Rose made Bobby freeze until the sheep got its confidence back. Then, just as if they were guided by the palm of a big hand, the sheep trotted sweetly into the pen and Rose clattered the gate shut behind them. The sound seemed to echo right over the top of the hills, up into the mounds of puffy clouds blowing in the sky above.

Mum was very pleased with Rose. She kept smiling at her and saying, "well done". They drove to school singing "Ten Green Bottles", with the car windows down and the spring air rushing in over their faces.

"And if one green bottle should accidentally fall…" sang Rose.

"There'd be no green bottles, hanging on the wall!" Mum sang back, smiling. The cold pool of bad feeling inside shrank to a tiny puddle; getting the sheep penned had made up, at least a little bit, for the puppy.

The car stopped outside school and Mum turned to look at her.

"I've been thinking," she said. "It's about time

you had a dog of your own to train." Rose's heart leapt.

"I was going to give you the best of Trix's pups," Mum's voice trailed off, her smile gone and last night's disappointment all over her face. Rose looked down at her school bag while the icy pool inside grew back to a lake. How was she going to tell Mum about letting Trix off the lead that day?

"Anyway," Mum began again. "I could buy you one of Bullet's pups instead!"

Bullet's pups would be perfect sheepdogs. Rose imagined a black and white silky head under her hand, and a dog called Shadow, or Lightning, running up the hillside at her command. But that thought only made the cold feeling worse, so Rose said something that even she found rather surprising.

"Don't buy me a dog. I'll train Trixie's pup."

Five

The first problem was what to call him. Border collie names just didn't seem right for a dollop of white fluff! But white fluffy names were no good for a working dog. For the next three months, while the pup grew and grew, Rose tried out every name she could think of.

"What about Snowball?" she said one evening over supper.

Dad groaned.

"We're not talking about names again, are we?"

"What about Killer?" said Robert.

Rose just stared at her brother; he was hopeless.

"Might help if you knew who the father was," said Dad.

"Well, that's just a mystery," said Mum. "There isn't a dog round here who looks even a bit like him. I can't think where Trixie found a mate like that." Mum laughed, a real laugh Rose was glad to see, and Dad and Robert were smiling too.

You couldn't really help smiling when you thought about Trixie's pup. To start with, there was the way he looked; like a giant, lollopy ball of wool, already more than half the size of his mum, and covered in perfect little cream kiss-curls of fur. He had all the energy of a sheepdog puppy but none of their excitability. He was always calm: "laid back", Dad said.

Everyone who met Trixie's pup loved him, and he loved them right back. In the morning the pup kept Mum company in the veg garden, or trotted along and sat beside Robert mending a tractor, or Dad doing the accounts in the farm office. He was always there to see Rose off to school and waiting at the gate, wagging his tail, when she came home. Nobody ever mentioned the fact that he was a mistake, not even Mum.

By the time the summer holidays came round, and Rose had time to try training her rather odd sheepdog, no one had to think of a name for him any more. He already had one that they all used: Puppy.

Puppy learned fast. He had two lessons a day, away from his mum. He learned "sit", "stay", "lie down" and "come", all in just a week. Rose got Mum out into the yard to show her what he could do.

"Puppy, lie down," said Rose. Puppy dropped onto his tummy.

"Puppy, stay," Rose said sternly, and left him at the bottom of the yard while she walked to Mum, standing by the back door.

"That's very good for such a young pup," said Mum. "Trix wouldn't have stayed so solid at that age." Puppy was still in the same spot, lying down as if he'd been glued. Rose was very proud.

"Puppy, come!" Rose called, and he leapt up at once and rushed across the yard like lightning.

"Good dog, Puppy. Well done!" She buried her face in his fluffiness. Mum fussed him too.

"'Well," said Mum. "I think we should show him the sheep tomorrow and see what he does."

Six

It was a chilly overcast day, with scrappy clouds like ripped grey socks rushing low over the hills. But it showed off the deep greens of late summer so beautifully that Rose didn't mind having to wear a sweater. Working sheep was better in the cool anyway.

Rose and Mum walked around the hill to the sheep with all three dogs – Bobby and Trixie free and Puppy on a lead, with his first collar.

"There's still a good bit of grass in this field," said Mum. "But it won't hurt to move the sheep into the next one. I'll work the dogs, you take Puppy up there where he can see and hear what happens."

"C'mon then, Pup." Rose pulled on the lead and Puppy came, looking over his shoulder at his mum, obviously not sure what was happening.

Rose took him quietly to the top of the field. Below them the ewes and their half-grown lambs, almost fifty sheep altogether, grazed in a loose gang. Puppy had never really seen sheep before, certainly not this close, and he was very interested indeed. He stared at them, his body tense, his floppy round ears pricked and his tail out like an antenna. The breeze began to blow in their faces. Rose could smell the sheep and she knew that the scent would be ten times stronger for Puppy, with his sensitive doggy nose. He lifted his snout into the air, taking long thoughtful sniffs and narrowing his big dark eyes. His expression reminded her of Mum reading the paper; he was fascinated! Rose's heart beat fast. Surely this was a sign that Puppy would be a great sheepdog!

Mum sent the dogs off, each with their own

whistled command. It had been a while since Rose had seen Mum working two dogs, and Trixie was a little out of practice. All the same, it was magical to watch. Mum could read the hillside like the pages of a book – the rolling dips and ridges of the field, the mood of the flock, the bodies of the running dogs. She directed her commands so well that Bobby and Trixie must have felt as if her voice was inside their heads. The dogs swirled gently around the flock, conducting them down the hillside towards the gate, like a dance.

Rose was so absorbed in watching that she didn't feel Puppy's lead slip from her hand. So, when a darting white shape appeared on the hillside, running straight for the centre of the flock, she didn't realize for a moment what it was.

There was no point trying to call him, the wind was blowing hard and would carry her voice away. In any case, she could see by the way he ran, with his tail out and his nose held forward, that nothing was going to stop him. Puppy was going to run right into the centre of the flock. They'd scatter and he'd chase them. It was a disaster! Mum would be furious.

But when Puppy reached the bunched flock, the sheep didn't take any notice of him at all. They stayed together and moved as Bobby and Trixie drove them, with Puppy in the middle of them, just like another sheep.

Seven

"Well, he isn't going to be much of a sheepdog if they don't even notice he's there!" Dad laughed when he heard the story of Puppy's first meeting with the flock.

"Maybe he'll learn to talk to them!"

Robert and Dad collapsed into giggles again. Rose could see that Mum wanted to join in, though she was trying not to.

"Don't take it to heart, Rose, love," she said.

71

"He's still a lovely dog, even if he can't herd sheep. I'll get you one of Bullet's pups like I promised."

"I don't want one of Bullet's pups," Rose shouted. "I want Puppy."

Rose got up from the table and stomped upstairs. Outside in the yard, Puppy was greeting Big Merv from the farm next door, waving his fluffy tail at him like a flag. Stupid dog, thought Rose. Didn't he know everyone was laughing at him? She shut her curtains and turned her radio on loud.

Rose didn't know how long she'd been asleep, but it was dark when she woke. The TV was on downstairs; Mum and Dad were probably dozing off in front of some boring gardening programme, and Robert was out.

She went down into the yard, where moonlight shone bright as day. The dogs had been shut into the loose boxes for the night and everything was quiet. But Puppy snuffled behind his door. Rose had been so angry with him that she hadn't seen him all day. He whined a little and Rose felt sorry. It wasn't his fault that he wasn't a sheepdog, like Bullet's pups would have been. She called his name softly and let him out. He wagged his tail and licked her hand. Rose took his lead off the hook by the door.

"C'mon, Puppy, let's go for a walk."

She took him down the lane, away from the fields where the Ridge Farm flock was, over the bridge and up the hill to the common where she could let him run.

Puppy was so happy to be out. He sniffed and snuffled at every plant and bush, and trotted beside her without once straining the lead. Mum was right, he was a lovely dog. Maybe it didn't matter that he was just a pet and not a working dog. Yet somehow Rose couldn't get that word *mistake* out of her head.

It was beautiful on the common: a wide velvet sky, and silvery hills off into the distance forever and ever. She sat in the grass and looked and looked. Puppy looked with her, his warm fluffy body leaning against hers, his nose lifted to read the air.

He was a good dog, and he deserved a little freedom before being shut up for the night. Rose got up and unclipped his lead. She walked a little way and Puppy trotted nearby, and then suddenly, out went his tail, up went his nose, and before Rose could say "Puppy" once, he was gone.

She searched up and down the common. She called, but not very loud. She didn't want anyone to know he was loose up here.

At last, she shoved the lead into her pocket and ran home, hoping no-one had noticed she'd been gone.

Eight

It was only just light when Rose heard the banging on the door. Mum and Dad must have heard it sooner, because they were both halfway down the stairs before Rose. The three of them opened the back door together. There was Big Merv, hunched in the early drizzle, with Puppy on a lead of string. Puppy was soaking wet and there was a blob of blood on his nose.

Rose felt sick. If Puppy had been caught chasing

sheep he'd have to be shot. That was the rule. But Merv was smiling, a big gap-toothed smile.

"Well," he said cheerily. "Great to have a welcoming committee. Guess what? Turns out your little mistake is a bit of a hero!"

Mum, Dad and Rose looked at each other, then back at Merv.

"You going to ask me in for a cup of tea or stand there with your mouths open like fish out of water?"

Merv had five cups of tea with two sugars, and a huge plate of toast and honey. He deserved it; he'd been out all night watching his sheep.

"I've lost eight lambs in the last week. I knew it was dogs. Strays, I suppose. So I've been keeping an eye out at night, watching the flock."

Merv took a big bite of toast and another swig of tea.

"Anyway, last night, the sheep were very quiet. Almost dozed off myself. Then just about first light, these two big mongrels come up, going for my sheep. And who pops up from the middle of the flock? Pup here! He must've been there all along and I just didn't notice him, and neither did the sheep."

Merv laughed.

"Pup got his teeth into one of the strays, then chased them over two fields. I've never seen two dogs more scared!"

Mum shook her head and smiled.

"Reckon you could do worse than breed a few more of him, Ruby!" said Merv. Dad slipped Puppy a slice of buttered toast when Mum wasn't looking; he winked, and Rose winked back.

Nine

It was still summer in September, so it felt weird going back to school. Especially a new school, with a bus to catch to get to it. Everyone came to the farm gate to see her off – Mum, Dad, Robert and Puppy, waving his big tail like a flag.

Rose walked down the lane to the bus stop. A girl in a new school uniform like Rose's was already there, with her mum. Next to them on the end of a smart leather lead was a dog, huge and white with kiss-curl fur. The girl said her name was Natalie; she seemed nice but a bit shy. Her mum wasn't shy at all.

"It's so nice to meet you, Rose," she said. "We've just moved in but we've met lots of people already. Everyone round here seems so friendly! Berja here made friends with a lovely sheepdog on the very first day we saw our new home, didn't you boy?"

Suddenly Rose found she couldn't say a word.

"I think sheepdogs always like other sheepdogs," Natalie's mum went on. "In Italy they use dogs like him to protect sheep from wolves, you know. Oh, now here's the bus…"

Rose and Natalie sat together on the bus.

"Sorry about my mum," said Natalie. "She's mad about our dog!"

Rose was staring through the gap in the curtains at the stars when Mum called in on her way to bed.

"Still awake, Rose?" said Mum.

"I've got something to tell you, Mum," said Rose in a small voice. "It's about Puppy."

Mum listened to the story of how Trixie had run off, and all about the big white dog at the bus stop, but she didn't seem cross at all.

79

"It sounds to me," Mum said, "as if Trixie knew exactly what she was doing. I think she knew all along that Puppy would be special."

Rose nodded.

"He is special, isn't he, Mum?"

"Very special," said Mum. "Just like you, Rose."

"But I thought I was a mistake."

Mum sighed and took Rose's hand in hers.

"It's true that we hadn't planned to have another baby," Mum said. "We thought we were just too old. And it was a bad time for the farm. We were selling the sheep and going to work on other people's farms. Dad and I were worn out and worried. And then you came, Rose. You came, and you were so sweet that you just made everything all right."

Mum smiled her best bird-bright smile and hugged Rose tight.

"Sometimes the things you don't plan are the best of all!" she said.

"Like Puppy," said Rose.

"Yes," said Mum. "Like Puppy and you."

The Mountain Lamb

One

It was the smallest lamb Lolly had ever seen. She put it in her bobble hat and carried it down to the shelter of the valley.

The stars were out by the time she got to the farmyard. Grandpa was in the barn with all the other newborn lambs and their mothers. Gently, he took the lamb from Lolly and looked it over.

"Never seen such a little scrap!" he laughed. "Reminds me of you when you were born!

Where'd you find her, Lol?"

Lolly didn't want to answer, but she didn't want to tell Grandpa a lie either.

"Up on the moor," she said.

"Hmm," said Grandpa. "You know Gran doesn't like you going up there alone." Grandpa frowned. His blue eyes always went ice-coloured when he was cross, and they were doing that now. Lolly looked down at her boots.

"Yes, Grandpa."

"But you did right to bring an orphan lamb in, where we can give her a chance."

Grandpa stopped frowning. His eyes thawed a bit and he plonked Lolly's hat on her head with one hand, so it slid over one eye.

"Better not tell Gran that you've been carrying sheep in your new hat!"

Lolly reached up and stroked the lamb, lying peacefully in the crook of Grandpa's arm. She could feel the tiny ribs beneath the silky nubble of baby wool.

"Grandpa," she said. "Can I keep her, for my own? Bottle-feed her and all?"

"It's hard work, Lol. A lamb's not a toy!"

Grandpa was frowning again now, eyes cooling. But Lolly was determined. She stuck her chin out and held her grandfather's wintry stare.

"I know about rearing lambs and I don't mind the work."

Grandpa sighed. "Hmmmm," he said. "Well ... I don't know..."

The lamb scrunched her eyes shut and snuggled her head into Lolly's warm palm.

"Please, Grandpa, please. She's like me: she's little and she's lost her mum."

Lolly looked up into Grandpa's eyes. They'd melted now to the colour of a summer sea.

"All right, my Lol," he said quietly. "But don't set your heart on her, she's very weak. If I can get her through the night, she's yours. Now run along in, and get your tea."

The farmyard seemed full of starlight as Lolly ran to the kitchen door. She *knew* her lamb was going to live. She just *knew* it!

Two

Lolly woke when it was still dark. She could hear
Gran in the kitchen below, clattering the big
kettle onto the range and tinkling the cups into
their saucers, ready for breakfast. Usually Lolly
jumped straight out of bed, but this morning she
wriggled back under the blankets. She wasn't so
sure about her lamb now. She remembered the
fragile ribs, the tiny nuzzling head. "Weak,"
Grandpa had said. "If I can get her through the

night," he'd said. *If.*

Lolly curled up small and pulled her pillow over her head. She didn't want to go downstairs to hear bad news.

Thump, thump, thump. Gran was banging the kitchen ceiling, Lolly's bedroom floor, with the broom handle, to call her down for breakfast. Lolly threw back the covers and scrambled into her clothes. You didn't wait for Gran to call you twice!

"Porridge is poured," said Gran, nodding her head to the table, where three full bowls sat under their little clouds of steam. Lolly slid into her chair, just as Grandpa came in from washing his hands in the scullery. She wanted, more than anything, to ask about the lamb, but she was afraid of what she'd hear.

Grandpa sat down.

"Mmmmm," he said. "Your Gran's porridge is hotter than the molten magma at the centre of the earth." He picked up his spoon and began to eat. Lolly searched Grandpa's face for clues about the lamb. His cheeks were red and polished from the cold air, but he looked tired. Was that a good sign or a bad one? She didn't know.

"C'mon, my Lol," said Grandpa, smiling. "Tuck in. Get some of that magma heat into you on this frosty morning!"

Grandpa was being very jolly. He must be trying to cheer her up. That was most definitely a bad sign. Lolly spread soft brown sugar over the surface of her porridge. At first it looked like sand, but in moments it melted into little pools and rivulets. Lolly pushed them with her spoon. She didn't feel like eating.

Gran sat down and poured them each a cup of tea.

"That's yours, Lolly," she said.

"Yes, drink up now," said Grandpa. "You'll need all your strength today."

What did he mean? Lolly blew on her tea, and looked at Gran and then at Grandpa. Gran's face was flat and empty, as it always was these days, but Grandpa seemed to be holding back a smile. Lolly couldn't work it out.

Then, she heard a tiny bleat. It came from a cardboard box tucked between the wall and the range. Lolly had been so busy expecting the worst news that she hadn't looked out for signs of the best.

"Maiiirrr! *Maaiirr!*" said the lamb. Her voice was too small to be loud, but it was very definitely demanding. Grandpa grinned.

"Madam wants her breakfast. You'd better see to it, Lol," he said. "She's worse about being kept waiting than your gran. Bottle's ready by the range."

Lolly had bottle-fed lambs many times before, but she'd never seen one so eager for her feed. This lamb planted her four feet, not much larger than pencil ends, and squared up to the bottle as if she were going to fight it! Even though her mouth was barely big enough to go around the teat, she sucked so hard that Lolly had to grip the bottle tight with both hands. The level of milk dropped fast, and the lamb's small stomach swelled visibly. As it did, her tail began to wiggle, faster and faster, until it was just a blur and Lolly had got the giggles. Gran and Grandpa both left the breakfast table to watch.

"I haven't heard you laugh like that in a long time, Lolly!" said Grandpa, and he looked at Gran and nodded.

"So," he said. "What are you going to call her?"

Lolly looked at the wiry little body, so tough in spite of its size, and without thinking any more about it she said, "Susan. I'm going to call her Susan."

No-one had said that name aloud for months. Suddenly the kitchen seemed very quiet indeed. Gently, Grandpa put his hand on Gran's shoulder. But she shrugged him off.

"The washing-up isn't going to do itself," she said, and a moment later she was at the sink clattering dishes into the bowl, with the radio turned up loud.

"That's a good name," Grandpa said gently. "I've always liked it. That's why we gave it to your mum." Then he put his boots back on and went out to the yard. Lolly took Susan in her arms and stroked her head until she fell asleep.

Three

Grandpa had been right. Rearing a lamb was hard work. Especially a lamb like Susan. She bleated for her food four or even five times a day. Each time, Lolly had to wash out the bottles and teats, and make up the feed from powdered milk and water. Susan butted Lolly's shins impatiently while she waited for her bottle, and jumped up so her sharp little hooves poked into Lolly's legs. She didn't like being left alone, either. As soon as she was strong enough to jump out of the box by the range, she began to follow Lolly everywhere, wriggling and squeezing her little bottom under gates and fences whenever she was shut in or left behind. Gran banned them from the house because Susan pooed on the floor, so Lolly and her lamb spent all day, every day, outside.

Lolly didn't mind a bit. Susan liked all the things that Lolly liked: playing chase, exploring, and making dens in the hay barn when it was too wet to be in the open. The lamb was such good company that Lolly would have slept with her in her pen in the barn every night if she'd been allowed.

Lolly knew that Susan wasn't really a pet, she was a farm sheep, and one day she'd be expected to join the flock and have lambs of her own. But every day Lolly pushed that thought to the back of her mind and went out to play with Susan.

The days began to lengthen. Gran didn't have to rub the frost off the porch window any more, and Grandpa stopped wearing his winter hat. Susan was eating hay and sheep nuts now, and only needed two feeds of milk a day. She had a sturdy body and tough little black legs, and she had grown too heavy for Lolly to carry.

"She's growing up fast!" Grandpa said one evening. He was leaning over the stable door, watching Lolly give Susan her last feed before bed.

"Another week or two and she won't need any milk at all …" Grandpa rubbed one hand through his hair, like he always did when he had something bad to say.

"So she'll be ready to go back with the flock, in time for you to go back to school."

Lolly looked down at Susan's madly waggling tail and at the last milk disappearing from the bottle.

"But she'll still need me," she said quietly. "Even when she's weaned."

"What she needs most, Lol, love, is other sheep. Same as you need other children."

Gran had marked the school terms and holidays on the calendar in the kitchen, even though Lolly hadn't been to school for months. Lolly watched the last few days of half term slipping away until it was the Monday morning that she was due to go back to school.

Lolly got up as soon as there was light to see with, to tend to Susan before school. The lamb knew the sound of her footsteps and started to bleat as Lolly crossed the yard to the barn. Lolly gave her a little pail of nuts and scratched the tight woolly curls behind her ears as she ate her breakfast.

"Come on," Lolly said. "Lets go for a walk."

It was cold and drizzly, and a wet mist drifted down off the moor tops in straggles, like wool caught on barbed wire. It closed in behind them as they walked up the track, so that the farm disappeared, and Lolly and Susan were all alone in a damp grey world. Lolly sat down on a rock and Susan began nibbling her coat and then her hair. The lamb's delicate little lips sorted through the strands of wispy brown hair, tickling Lolly's scalp, so she began to giggle, in spite of herself. Grandpa was wrong – she didn't need other children, with their talking and their questions about her mum. "Your mum fell off a mountain, didn't she?" they'd say. "Do you miss her?" Lolly shuddered. Susan was all the company she needed. For a moment, Lolly thought she would just get up and walk off

94

into the mist with the lamb. Then Gran's voice rang out through the stillness of the fog.

"Lolly! Lolly! Breakfast!"

She knew she had to try, because she'd promised Gran and Grandpa that she would.

Four

Of course, the hardest part was leaving Susan. The lamb didn't want to be shut into her pen again so soon and she called out "Maaiiiirrr!" again and again.

"She'll be just fine," Grandpa said. "I'll introduce her to the flock this morning. You wait, by the time you get home she'll be skipping around with a load of friends. Just like you will!"

Lolly tried to smile but found she was biting her

lip instead.

"Time to go!" Gran said. "Up you hop!" Gran opened the door of the Land Rover and Lolly climbed aboard.

Lolly hadn't been off the farm in months and months. The village was just down the hill, but school and other children were all part of the life she had lived with her mother. Since her mother had died, that life had become as distant as another planet. Lolly couldn't imagine herself in any part of it.

Lolly was glad today that Gran didn't chat, like she used to when Mum was alive. That they travelled down the hill in silence. She was glad too, that the fog got thick. It covered up the houses and the gardens that had once been so familiar, so she couldn't tell where she was.

Suddenly a big lorry loomed out of nowhere and Gran had to stop to let it get past. For the first time, Lolly took her eyes off the road ahead and glanced to her left. There, just showing in the greyness, was a little red gate. The house it belonged to was invisible in the mist, but Lolly knew every detail of it. The scent of the roses that grew in its garden, the way the front door stuck in rainy weather, the creak of its floorboards under her mother's foot.

The lorry stopped moving, pinning the Land Rover where it was. Gran got out to see what was happening. Lolly got out too and stood in front of the gate to her old house. She wanted to push it open, and run up the path and into the hallway. She wanted to find her mum, back from another adventure climbing in the Alps or the Himalayas, brown and skinny, unloading her pack onto the kitchen floor and laughing as Lolly hugged her. But she couldn't even touch the bright paintwork, she felt that the memories would burn her hand.

Lolly felt her eyes prickle and sting. She didn't want to stand there crying, so she squeezed past the Land Rover, ready to run back towards the farm. But there, in the middle of the road, was Susan, with Gran and the lorry driver chasing her.

"She must have got out!" Gran called. "And come straight after you!"

The lamb ran to Lolly, bleating. Lolly knelt down and let Susan's soft wool soak up her tears.

"Take us home, Gran," she said. "Please."

Five

Spring green crept slowly up the hillsides, colouring the hedgerows and fields, and spreading at last up and over the moor. Grandpa's sheep dotted the pastures, grazing in the sunshine, but Lolly's lamb wanted nothing to do with them. She wanted to go exploring, with Lolly or, sometimes, on her own. She'd learnt, on the morning Lolly tried to go to school, that she could jump out of her pen, and now there was hardly a fence or a hedge on the whole farm that could hold her. She went where she pleased.

"She's a mountain goat, not a sheep!" Grandpa laughed. He didn't seem to mind about Susan wandering all over the place. But Gran did. Susan had twice got into Gran's flower garden. The first time she ate all the primroses and the second time she trampled the snow drops.

"If that animal gets into my garden once more, I will eat her with mint sauce!" Gran said.

"I think she means it,"
Grandpa whispered. So he spent a
whole morning putting two strands of barbed
wire on top of the garden fence to keep Susan out.
That didn't seem to please Gran either.

"It looks like a prison camp!" she said, and went
back inside.

Susan spent the night in the yard outside the
kitchen door, but she woke every morning at four,
and baaed for attention. Grandpa always got up at
five, but Lolly knew he needed his last hour of
sleep. So Susan could not be left to bleat until
everyone was awake. Lolly had to get up every
morning and feed her. It was a good thing nobody
mentioned school any more, because by nine
o'clock, Lolly needed a nap!

Gran didn't want Lolly "running wild", so she had to do chores: housework with Gran in the morning and farm work with Grandpa in the afternoon.

The mornings were difficult. Lolly and Gran used to have lots of giggles over the housework, but now they didn't know what to say to each other. Usually, they ended up working in different rooms, each of them quiet and alone.

The afternoons out with Grandpa were lovely. He liked having Lolly with him, now that Gran didn't come and help with the sheep like she used to. They walked miles over the pastures and moors. Lolly loved watching the two sheepdogs, Flinty and Megan, working the flock to Grandpa's commands.

"Away, away to me", "come by, come by" and then, this mostly to Flinty who was still very young and excitable, "lie down, lie *down*".

Susan came too, trotting along like another dog. Sometimes she was useful in encouraging warier sheep to do what Grandpa wanted. She'd go into a pen if there were sheep nuts to tempt her, and the other sheep would feel safe to go in too, making the dogs' job much easier. But sometimes, there were awkward moments, when Grandpa had said "your lamb" twenty times in a row, to keep from saying "Susan", even once.

Sometimes, Lolly and Grandpa would look up from some job with the sheep, to find Susan had taken off. Grandpa said that she was just looking for some sheep she liked but hadn't found the right ones yet. But Lolly worried, and always went to look for her. Susan's boldness could get her into trouble.

Late one April afternoon, when the sky was gathering grey and the temperature was dropping, Susan vanished while Lolly and Grandpa were checking some fences.

"Leave her, Lol. She's probably run back down home. In with Gran's daffs I'll bet!"

"I want to look for her, Grandpa."

"We haven't got time, Lol. The vet's coming to look at that ram in twenty minutes."

"I can go on my own. She'll be stuck in the big bramble patch in the next field, like she was last time."

It had taken Lolly an hour to get Susan out of that tangle, and the lamb had lost a lump of fleece on the thorns.

"I don't know." Grandpa shook his head. "It'll be dark in an hour, and I don't like the look of this sky."

"Oh, please…"

"All right, but if she's not there, you must come straight back. You are not going further than the next field!" Grandpa's eyes went pale and stern. "Is that clear?"

"Yes, Grandpa," said Lolly. "Quite clear."

Six

Susan wasn't in the bramble patch in the next field, but Lolly was sure she'd be in her other favourite place, a thicket of gorse two fields higher, right on the edge of the moor Grandpa had been right to worry about the weather. Winter always had one last late fling up here, and now it looked like snow. Lolly knew how fast a blizzard could come down from the moor and drown you in blinding whiteness. You could freeze to death never knowing you were half a mile from home and safety. But that thought made her all the more determined to find Susan; she wasn't having her lamb out in a snowstorm overnight, even if it meant breaking her promise and taking a risk. Grandpa would do the same if he were missing a sheep.

Lolly looked into every hollow and dell of the thicket, all the places where the lamb had got herself stuck before. It took a lot of time, and when she looked up to check the weather again, her heart raced. The farm had gone, lost in a shroud of white that had spilled down from the moor on the other side of the valley. She looked behind her and saw that a blizzard was coming at her from above as well as below. If she ran down the field now, it would catch her in the open, where there was no shelter. Her only chance was to hide from the storm, the way a sheep would, buried in the heart of the thicket. She found a deep hollow full of gorse bushes and crawled in among them. She hoped that, wherever Susan was, she knew enough to do the same.

Almost at once, the blizzard closed over her

head, like a vast falcon swooping on its prey. Lolly heard the hit and rush of the storm's wings above her and felt the sudden icy cold of its breath. Snow as fine as sand filled the air, scouring every recognizable feature from sight. The white of the snow and the black of the falling night mixed to a swirling grey nothingness. Lolly crouched lower, hardly feeling the stab of the gorse needles. She folded herself up small, with her knees tucked into her coat and her hood pulled tight over her head and face.

Lolly had never heard the wind make noises like it did in that storm. It growled and shrieked around her so that she imagined some monster getting ready to grab her. The cold was intense. It sucked at her as she crouched in her spiny hiding place, drawing the heat and life out of her, no matter how she resisted. She felt the blizzard wanting to kill her and she was afraid, really afraid, for the first time in her life.

This was how her mother had died. Caught in a wicked, out-of-season storm, high in the Himalayas. She'd fallen almost two hundred feet. She had thought herself lucky to be alive and crawled into her tiny tent, like a caterpillar in a cocoon, to wait while her partner went for help. But the storm had come. Winds of a hundred miles an hour, blasts of ice particles like tiny razors in the air. Susan didn't give up. She fought. It took the storm three days to make her lie down and die.

"Never forget how much I love you," Susan had written on the last postcard she sent to Lolly. It got to the farm a week after the news of her death. It had a picture of a smiling sherpa on one side and Mum's big, loopy writing on the other. Lolly had pushed it to the back of a drawer. She had wanted to forget that love. So had Gran and Grandpa. Remembering it hurt too much. So Lolly had tried to forget about her life with Mum in the cottage with the little red gate. That life was lost and gone, and without it the world was grey and empty.

Lolly could feel the cold taking her, creeping up her back and across her shoulders. It had got her legs and arms already and was slithering into her belly and up through her chest. Soon it would take her heart. She felt sleepy. She knew this was bad. Her mum had told her once that it was the trick the cold played on you, to tempt you to relax so it could kill you. She tried to fight it, but her eyes were closing all the same.

"Never forget ..." The loopy handwriting danced before her eyes, and the sherpa smiled ... Quite suddenly, Lolly felt a sharp pain, as gorse prickles stabbed her body through her clothes. The numbness in her skin had gone, and now she was much too uncomfortable to sleep. Something inside her was pushing the cold back. A wave of warmth rolled up her tummy and lapped around her heart.

"Never forget how much I love you. Never *ever, ever, ever!*" her mother's voice whispered, in her head, and then there was another voice calling, faint through the wind's shrieking, and then stronger.

"Lolly! Lolly!" It was Gran!

A second later, Flinty was licking her face and barking fit to bust. And a second after that there was a blinding torch beam, and Gran scooping her up, easy as a newborn lamb.

"I never knew you were so strong, Gran."

"Neither did I, my sweetheart. Neither did I."

Seven

Lolly's lamb had come home on her own. Or not quite on her own. She'd made friends with the three wiliest old ewes on the farm, who lived all year high on the moor and only came down to shelter when the weather was at its worst.

"They walked into the yard as if it were a hotel," Grandpa said. "Your lamb took them straight into the barn!"

The story of Lolly's lamb and her new mates

was funny now, in the safety of the morning, with the land all covered with a quiet silver blanket of snow. But last night it had told Grandpa that Lolly must be in danger.

"When I saw those three old girls, I knew we were in for a bad night. And I knew you'd stay out looking for that lamb, while she was safe in the barn!"

Gran and Grandpa had gone searching for Lolly as soon as the snowstorm had struck. It had taken them almost three hours to find her.

"We couldn't see more than an arm's length in front of our faces," said Gran. "Nastiest bit of weather we've had in years."

"That didn't put your grandmother off," said Grandpa. "She wasn't with the Mountain Rescue for nothing, you know."

Gran had been with the Mountain Rescue! Lolly stared at her grandmother and then remembered to close her mouth. Gran laughed.

"I know, hard to believe to look at me now. But I worked with the Mountain Rescue for twenty-five years, bringing walkers and climbers down off the moors in bad weather."

Grandpa reached across the table and squeezed his wife's hand.

"Your mum got her talent for climbing from Gran, Lol."

Gran's eyes filled up, but she kept her head high and took a deep breath. Then she spoke very slowly and carefully, as if she were pulling each word up from a deep well.

"Yes," she said. "I made Susan into a mountaineer."

"And a fine mountaineer she was too," said Grandpa. Gran nodded her head and let the tears roll down her cheeks to the corners of her smile.

Lolly felt that her heart had just begun to beat again, after a long, long time of lying still and frozen.

"Maaaiirr, maaiirrr." A familiar voice called from outside the kitchen door. Lolly's lamb had brought her three new best friends to get some extra breakfast.

Eight

The snow didn't thaw for ages. All the children in the village spent Easter tobogganing. So when Lolly stood up in front of her old class in school, she could see two arms in plaster and an obviously missing front tooth.

Lolly was giving a talk. She wasn't nervous because she'd practised it in front of Gran and Grandpa, and they'd really liked it. She had lots of things to remind her what to say: climbing ropes

113

and pitons, ice axes and caribiners, and photographs of her mum smiling at the top of mountains all over the world. She even felt OK when she got to the part about how Susan had died trying to climb a very special mountain. But the most important part of her talk came right at the end, and she had to take it very slowly.

"I'm not sorry my mum climbed mountains, I'm glad," Lolly said. "I'm very proud of her." And then Lolly showed the class the postcard. She read the words in the loopy writing on the back and told her class how those words had kept her warm inside a blizzard.

"I will never forget how much my mum loved me. Not ever, ever, ever."

Then Lolly sat down, smiling, and everyone clapped.

It's the first day of Pony Camp at Merryfield Hall Riding School. Amber has been looking forward to it for months! But that evening, she spots a pony in a neighbouring field, being bullied by a group of boys. Told that his owner no longer wants Oscar, and that in the morning he will be taken away and destroyed, Amber is horrified, and hatches a rescue plan. But can she keep him hidden long enough to find the owner and convince him to save Oscar?

BY JUNE CREBBIN

"This has every ingredient for a brilliant read for the seven-plusses: magic, mystery and adventure."
Liverpool Echo

A small wooden elephant is gathering dust in an old house, dreaming of a white palace, when he's flung into an adventure and finds himself helping three children: Sara, a shy young musician, Nita, who has something to prove, and Jack, who's angry with his mum's new boyfriend. Leaving happiness in his wake and making several small, whiskery friends along the way the elephant goes on a magical journey across continents, and finally fulfils his own dream.

BY PENNY DOLAN

William Popidopolos is in a race against time in this comic adventure where mythology and reality collide!

William travels to a Greek isle to meet his long-lost father. There he meets a talking swan, who is really Zeus, king of the gods - and he desperately needs William's help. The knot that ties the world together is slipping, and the planet is about to explode! Can they trick the Gorgons and retie the knot before it is too late?

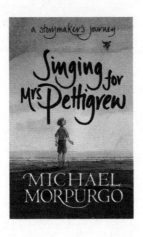

"From the first sentence of a Michael Morpurgo book, you know you are in the hands of a natural storyteller." *The Guardian*

This collection by the 2003-2005 Children's Laureate, Michael Morpurgo, contains short stories, essays and commentaries to illuminate the craft of storytelling. Analyzing all aspects of writing - character, plot, sources and inspiration, retelling and biography - it is perfect for anyone, young or old, who loves great stories and wants to know more about the art of telling tales.

BY MICHAEL MORPURGO